Double Trouble

As Neil walked through Kennel Block One, his footsteps on the concrete floor set off a series of welcoming barks from the various pens. There was the deep bass from Bumper, an enormous St Bernard, some higher-pitched barks from Carly, a Cocker Spaniel, and an assortment of other yaps and barks from the other boarders which included Alsatians and poodles.

But something wasn't right. There was a missing ingredient: no ear-shredding, high-pitched yapping from Sugar and Spice. Why were they so quiet?

Their pen was the last in the row. As Neil looked inside he could see why. Their kennel door was wide open and Sugar and Spice were gone.

Titles in the Puppy Patrol *Series*

More Puppy Patrol stories follow soon

Puppy Patrol
Double Trouble

Jenny Dale

Illustrated by
Mick Reid

A Working Partners Book

MACMILLAN CHILDREN'S BOOKS

Special thanks to Elizabeth Dale

First publication 1997 by Macmillan Children's Books
a division of Macmillan Publishers Limited
25 Eccleston Place, London SW1W 9NF
Basingstoke and Oxford
www.macmillan.co.uk

Associated companies throughout the world

Created by Working Partners Limited
London W6 0HE

ISBN 0 330 34908 2

Copyright © Working Partners Limited 1997
Illustrations copyright © Mick Reid 1997

15 17 19 18 16

A CIP catalogue record for this book is available from
the British Library.

Typeset in Bookman Old Style
Printed and bound in Great Britain by Mackays of Chatham plc, Kent

Chapter One

I f ever there was a subject Neil Parker couldn't stand last thing on a Thursday afternoon it was History. As he doodled strange shapes on his notepad, Neil's eyes kept straying to the clock on the wall. There were just five more minutes left. Five long, slow minutes until the bell would ring and he'd finally be allowed to escape from school, from Mr Hamley and from the worst subject in the world.

"The trade routes were a vitally important link at this time," Mr Hamley droned on, "and were responsible for more than just the widespread distribution of spices."

Neil suddenly sat up. Spices? Oh no! How could he have forgotten?

There were two West Highland white terriers coming to stay at King Street Kennels that night. Two very spoilt and badly behaved terriers called Sugar and Spice.

Neil shuddered as he remembered some of the things they'd got up to the last time they'd come to stay. They seemed to work as a team. One would stay put, tail wagging, head to one side, with eyes all big and innocent above a shiny black nose, while the other created absolute mayhem.

His mother had never forgiven Sugar for digging up her organic lettuces and using them as footballs.

Neil couldn't help but chuckle to himself.

He looked up to find that everyone was staring at him. So was Mr Hamley. The look on his teacher's face could have turned the sun to ice.

"And perhaps, Neil Parker, you'd be so kind as to tell us why you find the trade routes to China so amusing?"

"Um . . . well . . . the thing is . . ." Neil couldn't think what to say.

At that moment the bell rang and Neil heaved a sigh of relief. He knew that Mr Hamley had to get away quickly after school to referee a football match.

"You'll have to save it until tomorrow, then," said the teacher. "And at the start of the lesson you can explain foreign trade in the sixteenth century. Since you find it so funny, no doubt we'll all find your talk immensely enjoyable."

Neil's heart sank. He hadn't been listening to a word.

"Hard luck!" said Hasheem, as he walked

past Neil on the way out of the classroom. "What were you laughing at, anyway?"

Neil explained to his friend all about his sense of impending doom over the new arrivals. "They're not even here yet and they've already got me into trouble!"

"They sound wicked!" said Hasheem.

Neil grimaced. "They are. The annoying thing is that everyone thinks they're little white angels. You'd never guess they were complete demons!"

"Bet their fur doesn't stay white very long!" said Lucy Vaughan. She and her twin brother Jack were standing nearby. They always wanted to know about King Street Kennels and the dog rescue centre – even though they didn't have a dog of their own.

"It certainly doesn't!" Neil laughed.

"How *do* you keep white dogs clean?" asked Jack. Lucy's brother was more serious than his sister and always asking questions.

"Well, if they get really filthy, we give them a proper shampoo," Neil replied. Then he caught Mr Hamley's eye. How was Neil possibly going to talk about ancient foreign trade tomorrow when he hadn't listened to a word today?

"Can I borrow your notes from today's lesson, Hasheem?" asked Neil.

"Sure," said Hasheem. "They're not very good, though. My biro ran out of ink ten minutes ago."

"You can borrow mine if you like," Lucy offered, and held out her exercise book.

"Great!" said Neil. "Thanks very much."

"You wouldn't want to borrow mine," Jack said. "I write so fast that nobody can read my writing except me. Mr Hamley's always having a go at me about it."

Neil compared the two exercise books. Jack's was covered in unreadable scrawl. Lucy's notes were more neatly written and covered pages.

"Thanks, Lucy. I'll let you have them back tomorrow," he promised.

Neil rushed out of the school gate and saw the family's green Range Rover, with its distinctive King Street Kennels logo on the side. Neil loved the fact that his parents ran a boarding kennels. Wherever they went, people knew that they helped dogs.

As well as owning King Street Kennels, the Parkers ran a dog rescue centre where they tried to reunite strays with their owners, and find homes for unwanted dogs. All their friends called Neil and his family the Puppy Patrol.

Neil opened the car door, slung his bag inside and climbed in. His sister Emily was there before him, her head buried in an animal magazine.

Neil looked around. "Where's Squirt got to?" he asked.

"Squirt" was Neil's pet name for his younger sister. She was always late out of school.

"Look. There she is," said his mum, with a smile.

Neil turned and could just see Sarah's long black ponytail as she skipped out of the infants' playground. Unfortunately, there was a red setter tied up at the playground entrance and he knew that Sarah would stop and say hello to it.

"About time," grumbled Neil when Sarah eventually hauled herself up onto the back seat of the car. "School was awful today. I want to get home and see Billy. I don't

6

suppose anyone's come for him today, have they, Mum?"

Emily looked up hopefully.

Carole Parker shook her head. "I'm afraid not," she said.

Emily and Neil exchanged looks. Billy had been brought to the rescue centre several weeks earlier. He was big and black and very affectionate. Billy had only one eye and half an ear was missing. He had been very thin and bedraggled when he was found, but Carole and Bob Parker had nursed him back to health and now his coat was sleek and glossy. So far, the kennels had not been able to find a new home for him and time was running out.

"His two months are nearly up, aren't they?" asked Emily, anxiously.

The local council, who helped fund the rescue centre, had clear rules. Stray dogs could only be kept for two months. If no one had offered them a home in that time, they must be put down. King Street Kennels had never yet had to destroy a perfectly healthy dog, and Neil and his sisters couldn't bear to think about the possibility. Billy's time was up on Monday.

"You know who we've got coming tonight, don't you?" said Carole Parker.

"Sugar and S-P-I-C-E," said Neil in a horror movie voice.

"Oh no! Not them!" said Emily.

"Afraid so," said their mother. "It's only for the weekend, thank goodness! As usual, none of Mr and Mrs Jepson's friends or relatives would take them, so, like a fool, I said yes again. Poor things. It's not their fault they're the way they are."

"Do you think they'll be any better behaved this time?" said Emily. She had problems liking the dynamic duo.

"No chance," grunted Neil. He tolerated them. Just.

"They're lovely!" squealed Sarah, who plainly couldn't see anything wrong with Sugar and Spice.

"I think they should be your responsibility this time, Neil," announced Mrs Parker. "You've done such a good job with Sam. I'm sure you can keep Sugar and Spice in check for just one weekend."

"Do I have to?" said Neil. "Sam's different. He *wants* to behave well."

Sam was the family pet, a black and white Border collie who had once been abandoned and brought into the rescue centre.

"It's only for a weekend, Neil. And you know they need extra attention. I'm sure they'll be a credit to their owners come Monday."

"What? To the Jepsons? They're just as bad, Mum!" said Emily.

Carole Parker couldn't help agreeing as she drove out of Compton towards King Street Kennels.

"You're right! They're the ones who should be trained, not the dogs!"

Sam was the first to welcome Neil as he came out of the house and into the courtyard. The Border collie bounded alongside him as he headed towards the kennels. Emily and Sarah caught him up and all the dogs wanted to say hello as the children walked past each pen.

"Hello, you lot!" cried a tall, slim, blonde girl dressed in jeans and a sweatshirt. "School over already?"

Kate was the King Street kennel maid.

She looked up as she brushed out an empty kennel. Kate loved her job and always said that she was going to stay there until she could train the dogs to muck out their own pens.

"Getting ready for double trouble?" asked Neil.

Kate pulled a face. "Don't remind me!" she said, with a shudder.

"Don't look like that," said Neil. "You know Sugar and Spice are quiet, sweet-natured little things and you love them to bits, really."

"Not!" said Emily.

They all burst out laughing.

"I wish they were half as good as Billy. Have you seen him yet?" Kate asked.

"We're off there now," said Neil. "How's he been today?"

"No trouble at all," said Kate. "I can't understand why no one wants him."

Billy bounded up to the door of his pen in the rescue centre, barking a friendly welcome to his visitors. The dog was so excited he didn't know who to go to first. He licked Neil's hand, jumped up at Emily and then nuzzled Sarah's neck. Then he gave a little whimper and pricked up his whole ear, twitching the stump of his other one.

"Oh, I do love you, Billy!" said Sarah. "I wish we could keep you."

Neil looked at Emily over Sarah's head. They knew their dad had said they could never keep a rescue dog but they'd all got so attached to Billy. He'd been there so long and was such a loving dog.

"I'll ask Dad tonight," said Neil. "Who knows, maybe he'll agree. He's fond of Billy, too. I know he is."

"If no one else comes to get him, we'll just have to keep him, won't we?" said Sarah hopefully. She wiped her cheek with the sleeve of her woolly jumper.

Neil bit his lip. If he had anything to do with it, they would keep Billy. He would do anything to keep him at King Street.

Sugar and Spice were heard long before they were seen. Two piercing sets of barks rang out from the driveway in front of the house.

"I recognize those barks," said Neil grimly. He put down Lucy's exercise book on the sofa next to him. "History will have to wait. The terrors have arrived!"

Emily sprang up from her seat in front of the TV and disappeared upstairs with Sarah, leaving Neil to greet the new arrivals with his parents.

Mrs Jepson stood on the gravel outside, wearing a hideous pink dress that ballooned around her ample figure. She was holding two leads, one pink and one blue, both studded with pieces of shiny glass that shone like diamonds. Straining at the end of each were the two Westies, their fur brushed and back-combed. Sugar had a big pink satin bow tied between her ears, and Spice had a blue one.

Neil had never seen anything like it. The dogs looked ridiculous and were uncontrollable. He winced as Spice lifted his leg against the wheel of the Jepsons' car. Nobody told him off. Sugar jumped up and clawed at her owner's legs. Mrs Jepson's feeble reprimand of "Calm down, my sweetie!" did nothing to make the dog stop. Neil was going to have his work cut out keeping these two dogs in check. It could turn out to be the longest weekend of his life.

"Thank you so much for taking our two little babies at such short notice," cooed Mrs Jepson to Bob Parker. "They always love staying here, don't they, Norman?"

Mr Jepson gave a sort of snort which might have meant, "Yes."

The Jepsons were King Street Kennels' least favourite people. Mr Jepson was tall, bony and perpetually bad-tempered. He was a leading member of the local council and was known for his strict enforcement of council decisions, even if they were unpopular. He never smiled and hardly ever spoke.

Mrs Jepson was the complete opposite – all roly-poly and false smiles. Her hair was dyed blonde and hung in ringlets round her heavily made-up face, and she would talk for ever if you let her.

"We're going for a long weekend in Paris," she said, pronouncing it *Paree*. "We went to Venice last month, you know. So historical, so picturesque – all those darling little canals—"

Her husband interrupted, tapping his watch. "Time we were going," he said bluntly.

Mrs Jepson's pink-painted lips drooped at the corners. "Oh dear. Well, bye-bye, my darling babies," she cried, scooping Sugar and Spice up in her arms and kissing them each on the nose. "Mummy's going to miss you so much!"

She turned to Mr Parker. "Now you will feed them properly while we're away, won't you? Chocolate drops in the morning and cream every night. Oh, and they love cheese on toast. And chicken stewed in butter."

"I can assure you Sugar and Spice will have a good, healthy diet and be really fit and well for when you come back, Mrs Jepson," promised Bob Parker.

"Goodbye, my darlings!" she cried, dabbing at her eyes with a pink hanky. She climbed into her car and waved again through the window.

Neil smiled back through gritted teeth.

"Did Mr and Mrs Jepson ever have children?" he asked, as they waved them off.

"Sugar and Spice *are* their children," replied his mother.

"And are we *really* going to give them chocolate drops and cream?"

"Not a chance!" laughed Mr Parker.

"But you told Mrs Jepson—"

"—that Sugar and Spice would have everything they need," confirmed Mr Parker. "What they *don't* need is any of that awful cream and chocolate and cakes that Mr and Mrs Jepson give them. Look at them, they're far too fat already!"

The two Westies struggled on their leads and sniffed at any feet within reach.

"If these two didn't keep coming here for a proper diet and exercise regime every now and again, they'd be very ill! No, it's going to be proper dog food for these two from now till Monday. Whether they like it or not!"

Chapter Two

Neil took charge and led Sugar and Spice through to their pen in Kennel Block One. Barking loudly and tugging on their leads as they approached the main door, the two dogs refused to walk to heel and controlling them was not an easy task.

"They're impossible!" Neil cried.

Mr Parker opened the kennel door, and Neil ushered the dogs inside. Kate unclipped the leads and hung them up on hooks just inside the door. A chorus of barks and howls started up from some of the nearby guests.

"Noisy, aren't they?" said Kate, plugging her ears with her fingers.

"Let's get rid of those awful ribbons, Kate," said Bob.

Kate untied the two coloured bows attached to Sugar and Spice and smoothed down their rumpled bunches of stray hair. "There. You look more like real dogs now."

"Instead of toy ones!" said Neil.

"Let's see if you can start acting like real dogs, too."

"Work your magic, Neil," said Bob Parker, walking towards the exit. "I think lesson one has got to be getting them to walk to heel and stopping them jumping up at everybody."

"Can you quieten them down, too? They'll drive me mad otherwise!" Kate unplugged her ears and left for the store room to fetch some food and water bowls.

Neil watched the two dogs running around the pen, bouncing off one wall and then another in a cacophony of noise.

"Pigs might fly," he said.

"What are you going to say to Dad about Billy?" demanded Emily. She whispered her question to Neil, gripping his arm as she leaned across the kitchen table.

"Well, I'm not sure exactly what words I'm going to use," Neil began.

"That's why I need to talk to you. This is so important that we've got to have a plan." Emily always liked to have plans.

"Out with it, then," Neil insisted. "Dad will be here any minute for tea."

"List all of Billy's good qualities first. Then remind Dad how affectionate he is. And how much it would upset Squirt. He won't want to upset her because she'll go on about it for ages. Billy deserves more time. Surely Dad can see that?"

Neil shrugged. "I hope so," he said. "Anyway, here he comes."

Bob Parker and Sarah joined Neil and Emily at the table. Sarah began to turn her paper napkin into a dog.

"Mmm, smells like chicken," said Emily, sniffing the air as her mother carried a steaming casserole dish from the oven.

"A chicken special," Carole said. "One of my experiments. I hope it's worked."

As they tucked into their food, Bob Parker stole Neil's thunder. "Did you look in on Billy today?" he asked.

Emily shot Neil a sharp look. As Neil

opened his mouth to take a nervous breath before pleading for Billy's life, Sarah stepped in and ruined their plan.

"Oh, can't we keep him, Daddy, please, please?" she squealed.

Bob Parker looked at his wife and sighed. "Now then, Sarah, you know the rules. We can't keep every stray dog who is brought to the kennels, or we'd be completely overrun with them."

"I don't want every stray, I just want Billy," Sarah wailed. Her bottom lip started to tremble. "You can't kill him, Daddy. It isn't fair!"

"Don't upset yourself, Sarah," said Carole, stroking her daughter's hair. "We've never had to put down a perfectly healthy dog yet. Monday is ages away. People are far more likely to come and look for a dog at the weekend. We mustn't give up hope."

"We've done everything we can," said Mr Parker. "The vet knows we're looking. So do the RSPCA. Our advert in the evening paper will get some response too."

"Billy will make somebody out there a great pet," said Carole.

"If I was looking for a dog, I'd certainly want to give Billy a good home. But I'm not," Bob Parker said firmly. "Sam is more than enough for these four walls to cope with." He cast a meaningful look at a patch of scratched wallpaper, where Sam had recently been caught raking his paws.

"Billy will find a home, I'm sure," said Mrs Parker, with a comforting arm around Sarah.

"I need to think some more," said Neil. "I'm going to take Sam for a walk later."

"Are you taking Sugar and Spice too?" asked Carole. "I'll join you with Sarah." She cast a hopeful look in his direction.

"Sure. You coming, Em?"

"No way! I'm not going anywhere with those two!"

The evening air was warm and still. The nights were getting lighter and Neil knew that the summer holidays weren't far away.

Sam streaked through the trees, chasing the shadows and each small noise from under every bush. Neil followed behind with his mother and Sarah on their late evening walk through the woods. They had decided to risk letting Sugar and Spice off their leads and the two dogs were scurrying around excitedly, chasing each other and finding all kinds of interesting new smells.

Neil and Sarah threw sticks for them to fetch, but the two dogs were too busy sniffing at tree trunks and under bushes.

"I don't think they're usually brought anywhere wild like this," said Carole. "Mr and Mrs Jepson usually just take them on their leads around their housing estate or to the park."

"Poor dogs," said Neil. "No wonder they're sometimes uncontrollable. At least they seem fairly trustworthy off the lead."

Just at that moment, Sugar came scampering over to Neil with something large and black in her mouth.

Sarah let out a loud scream and buried her face against her mother's jacket.

It was a dead bird.

"Drop, Sugar – drop it!" commanded Neil.

The Westie took no notice.

"Drop!" Neil ordered, even more sternly.

Sugar turned her back on Neil, her tail wagging furiously, and proceeded to growl and fight the dead bird. Feathers flew in all directions and only a sudden sneezing fit from Sugar enabled Neil to kick the corpse away from her. He picked it up by one of the wing-tips. It was a crow.

"Poor birdy," sobbed Sarah.

Neil hid it in the branches of a tree nearby where he knew the dogs couldn't reach it.

To distract Sarah, Neil threw a stick for Sam. The Westies may have turned up their little black noses earlier at the idea of stick-fetching, but seeing that Sam was game too, they decided to join in. They shot past Sam, then careered back – the stick in Spice's mouth.

Sam managed to grab one end of the stick and began a frenzied, snarling tug-of-war with Spice on the other end. Sam was normally a gentle dog but when Sugar started snapping at his legs as well, he became much more noisy and excited.

Neil's mother stepped in. In her best sergeant-major type voice, she yelled, "Drop!"

Sam obeyed immediately, and ran over to Neil, but Spice refused to give up the stick. Carole Parker tugged at it but Spice pulled harder, his tail wagging like mad.

"Drop it! Bad dog!" yelled Carole, but Spice took no notice. The dog had obviously never been trained to fetch or drop, as the Jepsons had played very few games with either of them and had certainly never taken them to obedience classes.

Sugar gave a loud bark and Spice suddenly let go of the stick to bark back. Mrs Parker lost her balance and toppled over backwards into a patch of mud.

Sarah started to giggle but Neil was worried that his mother might have hurt herself.

It was only Carole's pride that was dented and she quickly got back to her feet. Neil could tell that she was still angry.

"I have never known two dogs as disobedient as Sugar and Spice," she said. "I'm never going to have them in the kennels again!"

"They're pretty terrible, aren't they?" Neil was quick to catch the dogs and clip their leads back on.

"Come on, let's get them back. I'm filthy!" Then Carole looked at Sam sitting at Neil's side. "Sorry, Sam, I know you wanted a longer walk."

"I'll take him, Mum. I'll see you back at the house later," said Neil.

"OK. Don't stay out *too* late, though."

Neil watched as his mother and Sarah walked back through the trees. He was glad to have Sam to himself. He gave the dog a good pat, then hurled another mossy stick as far as it would go up the snaking pathway.

"Come on, Sam," Neil shouted, after another ten minutes in the twilight. "Home, boy."

Having closed the gate to the field at the back of the kennels, Neil headed across the yard with Sam. As they passed the rescue centre, Billy barked another welcome to him.

He opened the main door and found Emily, kneeling down outside Billy's pen and talking to him through the wire meshing. She looked round when she heard Neil's footsteps.

"I've just been telling him what a lovely boy he is," said Emily, "and that we won't let him down." She sounded cheerful, but Neil knew Emily was very worried about what would happen to Billy after the weekend.

"Of course we won't let him down," replied Neil.

Emily turned back to look at the dog and Neil saw the remains of tears shining on her cheeks.

"We're going to try everything," he said.

Chapter Three

It seemed as though Neil had only been asleep five minutes when he heard the racket. He opened one eye and looked at his clock. It was ten to six.

"Oh, shut up, Sugar and Spice!" he groaned, putting a pillow over his ears to try to block out the sound. With a sinking heart, he knew it would not go away. Amongst all the other bad things about Sugar and Spice was the fact that Mr Jepson was a very early riser and usually gave them their breakfast around six. So now the overfed little monsters were hungry and making sure the whole world knew about it!

When he could stand the din no longer,

Neil got out of bed and went out to see the two Westies. They ran to the front of their pen to greet him.

"Hello, you little terrors!" said Neil, going into their kennel. "How are you today? Be quiet! Come on, behave yourselves."

He reached in his pocket, where he had a permanent supply of dog biscuits, and gave them two each. At least the little dogs had to stop barking while they were eating. Neil slipped away while they were busy. He quickly headed back into the house. He could take one last look at the history notes that he'd copied up from

Lucy's book. Wouldn't it be wonderful if Mr Hamley had forgotten all about Neil's talk to the class? He sighed. It was as likely as Sugar and Spice being good!

It was Neil's lucky day. As he and the rest of the class walked into the classroom, expecting another long Friday morning torture session, they were met by a jumble of electrical wires and equipment. Neil looked at it all and then at Hasheem, who shrugged blankly.

"Be careful where you walk! Don't trip over any wires, and don't touch anything!" Mr Hamley looked harassed. "Come on, class, settle down, we've got some important work to do this morning."

Neil looked at the microphone set up on Mr Hamley's desk and smiled. This was just the type of work Neil would enjoy.

"Right, everyone," said Mr Hamley. "May I introduce Tony Bradley?"

Neil looked at Hasheem. Tony Bradley?

Mr Hamley pointed to the corner, where a man, who'd been bending down fiddling with some wires, stood up.

"Hello, everyone!" he said.

As soon as he spoke, Neil recognized the voice. Tony Bradley was a reporter on their local radio station.

"Tony Bradley has asked if he can come along and interview you all for his radio programme, *Tell Tony*," said Mr Hamley. "I did tell you all about this last term, remember? For some reason, he seems to think that this class might have something interesting to say."

Everyone laughed.

"I'm sure you all have," said Tony Bradley. "As you know, we're always being told what other people think. Well, today I'm making a programme about what *you* think. I'd like to know what worries young people today – whether it's about the environment, world peace – whatever. So, if you could just sit and think for a few moments and jot down anything you'd like to say . . ."

There was an excited babble of chatter, as everyone talked about what they would say. Neil looked all around him. Everyone seemed full of ideas. But what did he know about world peace? He was thinking about a subject much closer to home.

*

Hasheem spoke first. "I'm worried about the starving people in Africa," he said, speaking into the mike confidently. Neil knew he would be much more nervous if he got a chance to speak. "It just doesn't seem right that I have too much to eat and they don't have enough. Why can't we share our food more? They can certainly have my mum's stew!" He pulled a face and everyone giggled.

"Well done, Hasheem," said Tony. "A serious problem put across in a humorous way. Who's next?"

"I'm worried about the ozone layer," said Jack Vaughan very quietly. "Every country knows that they should stop using the chemicals which are destroying it, so why are they being so slow doing anything about it? Don't they realize we could all die? My sister Lucy's got a worry, too. Go on, Lucy . . ."

"I've got a bike but I'm too scared to ride it on a lot of roads because of all the traffic," she said. "Our grandad showed us some photographs of the roads in the 1940s. There were hardly any cars on them and everyone rode bikes. Why can't we have separate roads for bikes and cars, so we can ride our bikes in clean air and not get run over?"

"An excellent point, Lucy, and one I wish the government would take on board throughout the country," said Tony Bradley. "Right, just time for one more."

Neil stuck his hand up.

"OK, Neil," said Mr Hamley.

"I'm worried," he said, speaking very close to the mike. "I'm very worried. I worry about all the things everyone has talked about. But the thing that bothers me most isn't in Africa, or outer space, or even in London. They're all too far away! There's suffering in Compton!"

Everyone had stopped fidgeting. All eyes were glued on Neil. Tony Bradley nodded encouragingly.

"My parents run a dog rescue centre, at King Street Kennels," Neil said. "We see all kinds of dogs brought in. Some of them have just got lost, but a lot of them are strays – abandoned pets. We have a dog in our kennels now called Billy. He's a mongrel. His owner treated him badly and then abandoned him. When Billy came to our centre, he was sick and weak and took a long time to recover.

"He's a beautiful dog. He's only got one eye, and half of one of his ears is missing, but he's the most loving, sweet-tempered dog you could wish for. My dad has done his best to find a new home for him. We all have. We've put ads in the paper and asked everyone we know if they'll take him. People have even been to look at Billy, but no one seems to want him. If he doesn't find a home soon, he's going to be put down. He's only got until Monday and then he's going to die."

There were gasps around the classroom.

"So what worries me," continued Neil, "is why are we so cruel to animals? Why do people have pets if they don't treat them properly? And why should Billy have to die, when he's never done anyone any harm and he's got so much love to give?"

There was silence when Neil had finished. A silence so sharp, so painful, that no one dared move. Suddenly, Hasheem started to clap and everyone joined in. Neil shot Mr Hamley a worried look. No doubt he'd be cross at him for going on about dogs again. But he wasn't and he clapped too. Mr Hamley smiled at Neil and nodded his head in admiration.

"Well done, Neil!" said Tony, slapping him on the back. "That was brilliant!"

Neil smiled at him. "Did I say too much?" he said. "Once I started, I couldn't stop!"

"No, it was excellent!" said Tony. "I couldn't have put it better myself. I shall certainly use it in the next programme. All of it."

Neil was filled with a warm glow. Maybe this would help Billy. Maybe, when *Tell Tony* was broadcast, someone would hear it and come and adopt Billy . . .

Just then, the bell rang for the end of the lesson.

"Right, class, I think we should thank Mr Bradley for coming in today, don't you?" With a scraping of chairs and desks, the classroom emptied. "And Neil . . ."

Neil froze in the doorway. "Yes, sir?"

"We'll forget about that talk on the trade routes, shall we? I think you've said quite enough already this morning!"

"Oh, er, thank you, sir!" grinned Neil.

"Well done, Puppy Patrol!" cried Hasheem, thumping Neil playfully on the shoulder as they walked outside. "Boy, you really 'Told Tony'! I can't wait to hear the programme go out."

Neil couldn't either. Then he had a sudden thought, and frowned. "Hang on, though!" he said. He could see Tony Bradley walking to his car just outside the school gates. Neil ran after him and shouted out, "Excuse me, Mr Bradley!"

"Yes?" replied the reporter, turning round.

"This programme," panted Neil, "the one that I'm on. When's it going to be broadcast?"

"On Monday evening as usual," smiled Tony, climbing into the driver's seat. "Bye!" And he slammed his door.

"Monday evening . . ." said Neil hollowly. But hadn't he been listening? Billy was going to be put down on Monday!

His bid to save Billy had been wasted. It would be too late.

Neil thought quickly. He reckoned his last big hope was Lucy and Jack Vaughan. He knew that they'd wanted a dog for a long time. Unfortunately, their mum didn't.

"She always said that our house was too small," said Lucy when Neil found the twins near the school sports hall. "But we've just moved into a bigger one."

"We could look after Billy ourselves and pay for his food out of our own pocket money," said Jack. "I'm sure she'd agree now."

"We'd take him for walks, we'd do everything for him," added Lucy. "We'd love to have him."

"Do you think your mum would let you?" asked Neil. "Really?"

"She's got to!" yelled Lucy.

"We'll ask her tonight," said Jack.

"Why don't we cycle home with you after school?" said Lucy. "Then we could see Billy and tell Mum all about him when we get home."

"OK!" agreed Neil. "You'll love him, you really will. He's gorgeous!"

"Oh, aren't they sweet!" cried Lucy, kneeling down and stroking Sugar and Spice in the courtyard behind the Parkers' house. Kate held on to their leads and had trouble keeping them calm even though they had just been out for an hour in the exercise field.

"They're such bundles of energy!" remarked Jack.

"Stop it, you're tickling!" spluttered Lucy, trying to get up. Sugar had decided to lick her latest friend.

"Come on, Sugar!" said Kate, picking her up. "This is no way to treat our guests."

"I think this one likes me," said Lucy. "What's his name?"

"Spice," supplied Neil. "Watch it. He's trying to eat the toggle on your anorak! Billy is much better behaved, I promise!"

Just then, Carole Parker pulled into the drive in the King Street Kennels Range Rover.

"Hi, everyone," she called, climbing down and lifting out two bags of shopping. Sarah and Emily followed her out, but when Carole saw Sugar and Spice, she briskly placed the bags back on the front seat. "I'm not getting these out till you've taken those two back to their pen," she said sternly. "There's food in here and I know what greedy-guts they are. They may look tiny, but they eat as much as two fully grown Alsatians!"

"Jack and Lucy have come to look at Billy," Neil explained to his mother.

"I hope you'll like him," his mother replied.

While Kate took the Westies back to their pen, Neil and the others went off to see Billy.

"Ah, he's lovely," said Lucy as soon as she saw Billy in his pen.

"Let's get him out to meet you," Neil suggested.

Although he must have been overjoyed at a chance to run round and stretch his legs, it was as if Billy realized instinctively how important this occasion was. Instead of rushing around the courtyard, he sat at Lucy's feet and let her and Jack stroke and pet him. When Lucy stopped stroking his silky head for a moment, he patted her knee gently with his paw and tilted his head to one side in such a winning manner that she crouched down and hugged him.

"We must have him, Jack," Lucy said to her brother. "I can just see him lying on my bed at night!"

"Do you think your mum will like him?" asked Neil.

"She'll have to," said Lucy. "She'll just have to. There's no other dog I'll ever want in the whole wide world!"

"Our mum will be back at five. We'll ask her right away," Jack told Neil.

"Ring me as soon as you know," Neil insisted. "I'll be waiting by the phone."

After they'd gone, Neil went up to his room, leaving the door open so he could hear the phone. He tried to do some homework but he kept glancing anxiously at his watch. Five past five. The twins should be calling him any minute now. Neil willed the phone to ring. But it didn't and time dragged by.

"Neil! Come and eat," called Mr Parker from downstairs.

Neil had just sat down at the table when the phone rang. He leapt up again and answered it.

"We can't have him," said Lucy's sad voice. "We told Mum all about him and she says he sounds too big for our house."

Neil gripped the receiver so tightly that

his knuckles turned white. "Did you tell her he's going to die? How good-natured he is? How well-trained?"

Of course they had. But by the sound of Lucy's voice, Neil knew there was nothing he could do.

Everyone had heard his side of the conversation and they looked bleakly at him as he walked back to the kitchen table.

"What are we going to do, Daddy?" asked Sarah. "Do you know how to save Billy?"

Mr Parker shook his head. Billy's future, which for a few hours had looked so promising, now looked as desperate as ever.

Chapter Four

Neil was woken very early on Saturday morning by the sound of what seemed like every dog in the kennels barking all at once. And loudest of all, as usual, were Sugar and Spice. He tried getting back to sleep but the dogs refused to stop barking. And Billy was on his mind too much anyway.

Feeling determined that today was going to be an action day he got up, dressed and went downstairs. His new plan was to confront people all over Compton with a photo of Billy and a request to give the dog a home and save his life.

Neil's mum was in the kitchen. "I wish

they'd keep the noise down," she groaned. "They've been at it for hours, you know."

"I heard!"

"Sugar and Spice have got such high-pitched yaps that it's giving me a headache. Take them out will you, Neil? Kate isn't here yet."

"Sure. I'll leave Sam and just go along the road," suggested Neil.

"OK. Thanks, Neil," Carole Parker smiled. "I'll have a big breakfast waiting for you when you get back."

Sam looked up at him eagerly as Neil moved towards the kitchen door.

"Sorry, Sam," said Neil. "I can't manage you *and* Sugar and Spice this morning. This afternoon, I promise."

Neil unlocked the gate through to the back of the kennels. As he walked past, all the dogs came forward eagerly to greet him. Sugar and Spice were the most welcoming of all.

"OK, OK!" cried Neil, as he clipped on their leads. "Be patient, will you?"

But Sugar and Spice didn't know the meaning of the word. They strained on their leads as he led them out of the

43

garden and on to the pavement in the direction of Compton. It was a bright morning and there was hardly anyone about. *Anyone with any sense is still in bed!* thought Neil.

Sugar and Spice sniffed and explored the roadside, tugging at their leads. They started yapping again without warning. Both of them pulled Neil towards the edge of the pavement. A blonde-haired young girl with a large golden retriever had just come round the corner on the other side of the road and Sugar and Spice were eager to make friends.

The golden retriever stopped and pricked up his ears, studying the two little white dogs. And then, suddenly, he bounded towards them.

The next few seconds seemed to happen in slow motion.

Just as the dog reached the middle of the road, a van came around the bend. There was a squeal of brakes and it skidded to a halt.

"Denny!" screamed the girl. "Denny!"

The dog had been hit and lay in the road, not moving.

A white-faced, middle-aged man in oily blue overalls climbed out of the van. Neil recognized him. Dave Thomas worked at the local garage.

Sugar and Spice were now very quiet. Neil checked that there were no other cars coming, tied the Westies' leads to a railing and ran into the middle of the road. The girl was already kneeling by her dog and crying as she stroked him. Neil was relieved to see that he lifted his head up and whimpered softly. He was alive!

"I just didn't see him!" Dave said. "I turned the corner and he was there, right

in front of me. I didn't have a chance. Thank goodness I wasn't going very fast. I tried to swerve, but there wasn't enough time." His hands shook as he reached out to Denny. The friendly mechanic had lived in Compton all his life and knew the Parkers quite well.

"I don't think he's too bad," said Neil.

"It's all my fault," sobbed the girl. Gina Ward was in a class below Neil's at Meadowbank School. "I should have kept tighter hold of him. He just yanked the lead out of my hand!"

"We'd better move him," Dave said. "He's not safe lying here."

"No!" said Neil, sharply. "Moving him is the worst thing we can do. He might have injured his back and a move could kill him. What we need to do is cover him with something warm. Have you got a blanket in your van?"

"I've got some sacks, I think," he said, going to look.

"And could you ring the vet?"

It was still early but Mike Turner was already out on a call. "I've left a message," said Dave apologetically. "That's all I could do. He'll be here as soon as he can. I'd better check there's no traffic coming."

"Can I ring my dad on that?" asked Neil, pointing to the mobile phone Dave was holding. Neil punched in the number for King Street Kennels.

"Dad, there's been an accident on Compton Road," said Neil, seconds later. "Just by the big bend. A dog's been injured. Can you get here quickly?"

Neil gazed anxiously at Denny. The dog was still whimpering, but he didn't lift his head any more. Was he growing weaker? Was there anything else Neil could do for him?

Finally, Mr Parker arrived. He parked the Range Rover so that it shielded Denny from any traffic coming in the other direction and knelt down to examine the injured dog. A few moments later he looked up.

"I don't think he's too badly injured," he said.

Neil heaved a huge sigh of relief.

"Neil knew just what to do," said Dave. "He told me not to move him, just cover him up."

"Well done, Neil," replied his dad.

"Yes, thanks so much," said Gina, managing a smile for the first time.

"We left a message for Mike Turner," Neil told his dad. "Was there anything else I should have done?"

"No, you did everything you could," said Mr Parker.

"I felt so helpless," said Neil.

"We all did," said Dave. "But you were brilliant, Neil."

Sugar and Spice reminded Neil they were still there with a couple of quick yaps.

"I think you'd better take them back to the kennels," said his dad, turning round and spotting the two Westies at the roadside. "There's nothing else you can do now, anyway. I'll wait here for Mike with Gina then run her home."

Neil frowned. He wanted to stay and hear what the vet had to say, but he knew his dad was right. "OK," he said. "I hope Denny will be OK, Gina. Please ring as soon as you get any news."

Neil kennelled Sugar and Spice as soon as he returned home and then headed straight for the office.

"Neil?" asked Mrs Parker, looking up from her desk. "Are you all right?"

"I'm fine, Mum."

"I hung on for you before I took Sarah out to her ballet. What happened?"

Kate stuck her head round the door. "Neil, I heard there was a dog in an accident."

Neil told them what had happened.

"How awful!" said Kate. "You've got to be so careful when you're taking a dog out for a walk, especially along a main road."

"It wasn't even busy," said Neil. "Denny was just unlucky. Sugar and Spice were quite upset."

"Sounds as though they've recovered now, though," said Kate, as she opened the back door and the familiar yapping sound could be heard coming from the kennels. "I'll see you later. Glad you're OK."

"Ready for your breakfast?" asked his mum. "It's waiting for you in the house."

"I couldn't eat a thing," said Neil. "Not until I know if Denny is going to be all right."

Just then the phone rang on Mrs Parker's desk. Neil looked at his mum anxiously.

Mrs Parker picked it up and listened to the caller. "Good," she said. "Fine. Right, I'll tell him."

She put down the phone and smiled. "That was Mike Turner. He's given Denny a good look-over and he thinks he'll make a full recovery. Your dad and Gina are at the surgery with him now. Everything's looking good."

"Brilliant!" grinned Neil. "I'm ready for that breakfast now. All of a sudden, I'm starving!"

After his breakfast, Neil joined Kate in the kennels storeroom. She was filling feeding bowls with food and others with fresh water.

"I've finally got some peace," she said, scooping up another handful of crunchy meal from a large sack. "The terrors have stopped – so all the others have too."

"They were very good while they were out with me. I think they were shocked by what happened. I'm sure dogs know when another dog is in pain."

"I'm sure they do," Kate agreed.

"I'll just go across and check them out."

As Neil walked through Kennel Block One, his footsteps on the concrete floor set off a series of welcoming barks from the various pens. There was the deep bass from Bumper, an enormous St Bernard, some higher-pitched barks from Carly, a cocker spaniel, and an assortment of other yaps and barks from the other boarders, which included Alsatians and poodles.

But something wasn't right. There was a missing ingredient. No ear-shredding, high-pitched yapping from Sugar and Spice. Why were they so quiet?

Their pen was the last in the row. As Neil looked inside he could see why. Their kennel door was wide open and Sugar and Spice were gone.

Chapter Five

"**K**ate, Kate!" Neil cried, running back across the courtyard. "Where are you?"

There was a clatter of dog bowls and Kate appeared in the store doorway. "What's the matter?" she cried, alarmed at the panic in his voice.

"Sugar and Spice!" Neil shouted. "Their kennel door was open. They've gone!"

"What?" Kate stared at him open-mouthed. "They can't be!"

Together they ran back into the kennel block. Kate couldn't believe it. There was nothing there except two empty dog baskets.

"I can't understand it," said Kate, looking around anxiously. "They can't have unhooked the door themselves."

"Their door was open, just like it is now," said Neil.

"You did shut it properly when you brought them back from their walk, didn't you?" Kate queried.

"I'm sure I did," he insisted. "I always do."

Neil's heart sank. If Sugar and Spice had escaped and something happened to them, he'd never forgive himself.

Kate gave Neil a worried look. "Let's hope nothing nasty has happened. They may just have got free somehow and be running around."

"We've got to do a thorough search," said Neil.

"I'll look around here, the house and the garden. You check the fields."

"I hope they're not in the house!" exclaimed Neil in alarm. "If they've got up to anything in there, Mum would never forgive me. I'd be grounded for weeks!"

There was no sign of the two lost dogs in the field that bordered the back of the kennels. Neil climbed on a fence and scanned the surrounding area. Nothing.

He met Kate back in front of the office. She shook her head and stood with her hands on her hips in exasperation.

"We've got to find them quick!" said Neil. "Before they get too far."

"I can't leave the kennels to search for them," said Kate. "Your parents are both out. I'm here on my own."

"I'll ring Chris," said Neil. "He'll help me look."

Neil opened the back door of the house. Emily was sitting at the kitchen table in her pyjamas.

"Em! Sugar and Spice are missing!" he said.

"I know," she replied. "Kate thought I might have them in here. No chance of that! What happened, anyway?"

"We're not sure. Their door was open and they'd vanished. It's a mystery. I'm going to go out on my bike, looking for them. Chris will probably come with me. I'll phone him now."

"I suppose you want me to help? I'll take Sam over to the woods if you like. If you took them up there on Thursday night, they might have remembered and wanted to go back."

Emily spooned some more cereal into her mouth, then pushed her bowl away. "I'll go now."

"We must try and get them back before Mum and Dad come home."

"Too right! There'll be trouble otherwise. Losing dogs is *not* good!"

Neil rang Chris Wilson and met him at his house a little further along the road towards Compton. They'd been friends for ages and went to the same school. Chris might be more interested in football than dogs, but he was always willing to help out.

"It's all my fault," said Neil. "I can't have shut their kennel door properly." He also told Chris about Denny's accident.

"What gives me the feeling that you're not having a good day?" said Chris. "Look, cheer up. Sugar and Spice can't have got that far, they've only got little legs."

"You're right." Neil forced a smile. "We'll find them, I'm sure. They're quite distinctive, after all. We'll probably hear them before we see them!"

"I bet I know where they are," said Chris. "You know what a homing instinct dogs have – they'll be heading for their house. You said their owners really spoil them with sweets and things, didn't you? They're probably fed up with healthy rations and want a few luxuries!"

Neil's face brightened. "You're right!" he said. "Can I use your phone? I'll ring Steve. He lives near the Jepsons. I'll ask him to look out for them."

Steve Tansley was Neil's cousin. He owned a Labrador called Ricky who was a regular at the King Street obedience classes.

"I wonder how dogs can find their way home," said Chris.

"Don't know," said Neil, heading inside. "But they do it in films! They follow a scent for hundreds of miles, over mountains, deserts, raging rivers – anything!"

Neil returned a couple of minutes later.

"He's going to keep an eye on the Jepsons' house for us. If they turn up while we're out, he'll ring the kennels and leave a message with Kate."

"We'll have a go at hunting them down, as well," said Chris. "We can't waste any time!"

The two friends jumped on their bikes and raced down the drive.

"Which way shall we go?" Chris shouted to Neil.

"Down the Compton Road into town. It goes to their house almost in a straight line. If those dogs have got any sense of direction, that's the route they'll take. They might have gone through the fields though. If so, we should be able to spot them. Good job they've got white fur!"

Searching thoroughly, they followed the road into the centre of Compton. Neil scoured the hedgerows on one side of the road, Chris carefully checked the other side, and from time to time they stood up on the pedals and craned their necks to see over the hedgerows into the fields.

"Sugar!" called Neil, hoping that the dogs would recognize his voice. "Spice!"

There were plenty of birds, singing their hearts out in the spring sunshine, and rabbits in almost every field. But no Sugar and no Spice.

Then they heard the sound of a dog barking in a roadside field on the outskirts of the town and both scrambled off their bikes to look. But it was only Dr Harvey taking Sandy, his light-brown mongrel, for a walk. He waved to Chris and Neil when he saw them peering over the hedge.

"Have you lost something?" he called.

"You haven't seen any West—" began Chris.

"—any stray dogs, have you?" Neil interrupted him.

"No." Dr Harvey shook his head. "But I'll call your dad at the rescue centre if I do."

"Why didn't you let me tell him we're looking for Spice and Sugar?" asked Chris, as they got back on their bikes.

"Because he's very friendly with Mr and Mrs Jepson," said Neil. "We don't want him telling them we lost their dogs while they were away!"

"But what if we don't find them?" said Chris, pulling a face.

"Don't even think about it," Neil replied.

Neil and Chris searched Compton without catching a glimpse of the Westies, and ended up by the park. Wheeling their bikes, they went inside and looked at all the dogs which were around with their owners. There was nothing small and white.

"Where to now?" asked Chris. He leant against his handlebars, tired after searching for so long.

Neil was tired too and shrugged. "Let's hope that they decided to go straight on home. Come on, the quickest way from here will be down Brown's Lane."

"Let's call in and see Steve," Chris suggested. "He could be our best hope now."

There was nobody at home. They cycled to the Jepsons' house to see if Steve was there, but the place was deserted. There was nothing for it but to admit defeat and go back home.

It was during the cycle ride back that Neil realized he'd been missing something all along. Something that could be vital.

"I've just had a brainwave, Chris!" Neil exclaimed, braking suddenly and screeching to a halt.

Chris shot past him, braked, and walked his bike back to where Neil was standing.

"Ever since I saw that empty pen at the kennels, something's been worrying me. There was something not quite right about it – and it's just dawned on me what it was!"

"Well, go on," Chris encouraged him.

"They had their favourite toys in the kennel with them. Sugar had a pink, squeaky mouse and Spice had a blue rubber ball. They weren't there. You can't tell me two dogs would run away and take their toys with them?"

"What are you getting at, Neil?"

"I think Sugar and Spice were stolen!"

Chapter Six

Neil and Chris cycled straight back to King Street as fast as they could.

Emily came rushing out of the house to greet them. "Kate says can you go and see her in the office as soon as you get back," she cried. "I didn't have any luck in the woods but she says one of them has been found!"

Neil set off through to the back of the house, followed closely by Chris.

Kate stuck her head out of the kennels office when she heard them approach. "There you are. I need your help because I'm still on my own," she said, running a hand through her long, blonde hair.

"Emily said one of them has been found. Which one?" asked Neil.

"That's just it. I don't know," Kate replied. "All I've had is a phone call from Badger's Farm."

"Great! You don't need to trouble Dad, we'll go and get him. Or her," said Neil. "Don't worry, Kate. Whichever one of them it turns out to be, the other one won't be far away."

Kate sighed and looked troubled. "There's more to it than that," she said.

"What is it?" enquired Neil, his relief at having found one of the dogs instantly dampened by the tone of her voice.

"The dog's in a bad way. It had caught its leg. That's why Mrs Rose rang. She didn't know about Sugar and Spice being missing – she rang to use our rescue service."

"How bad is the dog?" asked Chris.

"I'm not sure," Kate told them.

"We'll go straight over there," said Neil.

Even though Sugar and Spice were little monsters, one of them was suffering, and Neil couldn't bear to think of any animal in pain, especially a dog.

*

Neil and Chris dropped their bikes at the main farm gate and ran up the uneven and furrowed path that led to the farmhouse. Neil hammered on the front door.

Mrs Rose's anxious face, framed with grey hair, popped through the window. When she saw who her visitors were, she scuttled to the door and opened it.

"Thank you for coming so quickly, Neil."

"Don't worry, Mrs Rose," said Neil. "Where's the dog?"

"He's just through here in the kitchen getting warm."

Neil almost couldn't bear to look. Curled up on a blanket in front of the warm cooker was a very sorry-looking bundle of dirty grey fur.

"Which one is it, Neil?" Chris was bending down and peering at the tiny dog's face. Neil knelt down beside him and gently stretched out a hand. The frightened dog lifted up his head and turned it towards the two boys.

Neil and Chris stared at him, and then at each other.

It wasn't Sugar or Spice.

It wasn't even a West Highland terrier. It was a small, frightened little cairn.

Neil carried the dog into King Street Kennels and shouted out for Kate. Chris walked behind, pushing both bikes.

"Where's the patient?" asked Kate, rushing out from the rescue centre.

She looked at the little bundle cradled in Neil's arms and had a quick look at the dog's injuries. His paw and his leg were cut and bleeding, but apart from that, he seemed to be all right.

"He can walk OK, so I don't think anything is broken," said Neil. "I carried him all the way back just to be sure, though."

"There, there, don't worry, little feller," said Kate, as the poor dog whimpered when she tried to stroke his head and comfort him. "We'll soon have you in the kennels, nice and safe, then we'll see if we can get you better and find your owner."

"Do you recognize him?" asked Chris.

Kate shook her head. "No. He doesn't have a name tag, either," she said. "I expect someone will claim you soon, though, won't they? You're so adorable!

"I'll go and put him on a warm hot water bottle and towel and make sure he's comfy before your dad gets here," she told Neil, walking back towards the rescue centre. "I expect he'll want to take him to the vet. Cheer up! I don't think he's that bad."

"No," said Neil, "I wasn't thinking about him. It's Sugar and Spice. I was so sure we'd found them."

"Neil reckons they've been stolen, Kate."

"All their toys were missing too, remember?" added Neil. "Don't you think that's odd?"

"Very," said Kate, scratching her head. "I wonder . . ."

"What?" asked Neil.

"Well, when we first discovered Sugar and Spice were missing this morning, I went to look for them at the front of the house. Anyway, the gate was open. I'd definitely shut it behind me when I came to work. I always make sure I do, just as an extra barrier in case a dog gets loose in the kennels."

"You think somebody else left it open?" said Chris.

"Yes, someone must have come through the gate when I was in the office talking to you and your mum."

"To steal Sugar and Spice," said Chris, grimly.

"Do you remember? Sugar and Spice made that great big din," said Kate. "We thought it was because they'd suddenly recovered from seeing the accident. But I don't think it was that at all. I reckon they were welcoming someone who'd just gone into their kennel."

"But why take Sugar and Spice?" Neil said. "Do you think the thief was after any dog or just them in particular?"

"If anybody just wanted them, at least it probably means they're being well looked after," said Kate. "They aren't running wild and hungry, or caught in a trap . . ."

". . . Or being run over," added Neil, remembering Denny.

"If they were deliberately stolen, then the thief opened their kennel himself, so it wasn't your fault they've gone missing," said Kate. "You can stop blaming yourself."

Neil should have felt better. But he didn't. The Jepsons were coming back for Sugar and Spice tomorrow evening. He had just twenty-four hours in which to hunt for them and get them back. And they could be anywhere.

Just then, there was the sound of a car in the driveway. Neil and Chris ran to the front of the house. It was Mr Parker.

"Oh, Dad!" cried Neil, as he climbed out of the Range Rover. "Something's happened to—"

"I know," Bob Parker interrupted. "Kate rang me on my mobile. But I don't understand – how on earth did they get out?"

"Maybe someone took them because they look so cute," said Kate. "They are very pretty dogs. No stranger could know how badly trained and disobedient they are."

"They're not valuable," Bob pointed out. "We have prize-winning pedigree dogs staying here who are worth far more. The thief would have had to walk right past them to get to Sugar and Spice. And what was a thief doing hanging around on a Saturday morning, anyway? They were really lucky not to be seen. A professional wouldn't risk it – he'd come at night or on a weekday, when there are fewer people around."

Neil looked at Chris and shrugged.

"Anyway, I must ring the police if we suspect Sugar and Spice have been stolen," said Mr Parker. Then he frowned. "If only they'd been identi-chipped."

"What's that?" asked Chris.

"It's a way of keeping track of your dog," Neil explained.

"You can insert a tiny micro-chip, about the size of a grain of rice, under their skin," his father added. "If the dog is found by anyone, a scanner can be run over their chip and it will identify the dog. I did recommend it to the Jepsons but they wouldn't hear of it. Mrs Jepson was convinced it would hurt them. Besides, she said, they took such good care of them, there was no way their darling babies could possibly go missing."

"The police might just spot someone exercising them, I suppose," said Neil as his father went into the office.

Neil heard a familiar barking sound. Sam bounded eagerly up to him, his ears pricked and his big pink tongue lolling out of his mouth.

"Hello, Sam!" he called, bending down and stroking his dog. He looked up as Emily ran towards him.

"We didn't find them!" she panted. "I've been out again but couldn't see any sign of them. Any news here?"

Neil updated his sister.

"To think someone came right in here and just stole them," she said, looking over her shoulder. "It's really creepy!"

Mr Parker came out of the office.

"The police know we're looking for them now," he said. "There's not much else they can do."

"There must be something else *we* can do, though," said Neil. "I can't just sit indoors, waiting for the police to ring . . ."

"We'll go and have a drive around when your mum gets back," said Bob Parker. "In the meantime, what about that little cairn?"

"I brought him back from Badger's Farm," said Neil. "Come and see."

They hurried round to the rescue centre, where the cairn lay on a soft blanket in a basket.

"Oh yes, it's not nearly as bad as I feared," said Bob Parker, checking over the frightened little dog. "We'd better pop him down to Mike Turner's when we go out, just to make sure. We can see how Denny is getting on at the same time.

"He's got a broken hind leg, and a nasty cut on one of his front legs, but he's going to be all right," their father went on. "Mike wants to keep him in for observation tonight, just to be sure there are no other problems."

"Some good news at last," said Neil. "Is Gina OK?"

"She's still upset. I took her home to her mum and dad on the way back."

Just then Sarah came running up. She'd just got back from her ballet lesson. As soon as she saw everyone near the rescue centre, she danced over to them, twirling and skipping.

"Miss Hodgson says I could be a ballerina when I grow up," she said. "If I practise." Sarah twirled around and nearly fell over.

"Why is everyone looking so serious?" asked Carole Parker, walking up to them.

"Sugar and Spice have been stolen," said Neil.

"They haven't!" gasped Sarah.

"Oh no!" cried Carole Parker. She looked absolutely horrified.

"It's looking unlikely that we'll find them, too. Everyone has looked in all the obvious places already," said Bob.

"Once the thieves see how bad those two dogs really are, they won't want to keep them much longer, that's for sure!" Emily laughed at her own joke.

Neil knew she was right. The thieves *would* grow tired of Sugar and Spice, soon enough. But they wouldn't bring them back, would they? They'd be more likely to do something far worse.

As they were all walking back inside the house the phone rang and Neil rushed to answer it.

"Hello? King Street Kennels." Neil's voice was very quiet. He was anxious that it might be news he didn't want to hear.

"Hang on a moment, please," he continued. Placing a hand over the mouthpiece he shouted into the kitchen above the noise of the talking. "Ssh," he whispered. "It's the Jepsons!"

Chapter Seven

"How are my babies?" cooed Mrs Jepson. "Not giving you any trouble, I hope?"

If you only knew how much! thought Neil. "None at all," he told her.

"Are my bootiful-wootifuls missing their Mumsie?"

Neil gritted his teeth. "I'm sure they are. Lots!" he said.

"Well, give them a choccy-woccy, won't you, and tell them it won't be long before I'm home. Give them each a big kiss, won't you?"

There was some muttering, then her husband took over the telephone. "We'll be back around six tomorrow, traffic permitting," he said. "Goodbye."

Neil walked back to the living room feeling very uncomfortable about having lied to the Jepsons. "It was awful," he told his family. "I wish they'd gone away for a week, not just a weekend."

"We must do all we can to find them," Mr Parker said quietly. "Otherwise I wouldn't put it past Jepson to make life difficult for King Street Kennels."

"What could he do?" gasped Emily.

"He's on the Council. He could convince them that we're careless and negligent in letting dogs escape, or be stolen. We've got to be very careful." He stood up and shrugged. "Well, better get on. Let's get the cairn to the vet's, and see if we can spot Sugar and Spice while we're about it . . ."

Neil, Sarah and Emily went along with him in the Range Rover and stared out of the windows, hoping to see the two terrors looking out from a house or scurrying down the street. But there was no sign of them. On the way, they picked up Gina, so she could see how Denny was getting on.

The golden Labrador looked so much

better than he had that morning. He was wearing a big plastic collar, one of his legs was in a huge plaster cast and he had stitches all down a wound on another. With an excited bark, his eyes shining and his big pink tongue hanging out, he ran forward eagerly on three legs to meet everyone, saving his biggest noise of all for Gina.

"Hello, boy!" cried Gina, fondling his ears. "How are you, then?"

"What's that thing round his neck?" asked Sarah.

"It's a special collar to stop Denny nibbling at his stitches and undoing all my good work," Mike Turner, the vet, explained. "I'll leave you with him while I examine this other patient you've brought me."

"Do you recognize him?" asked Neil.

The vet lifted up the grubby cairn's chin, then stroked him gently behind the ears.

"No," he said, "I don't think so. Does your leg hurt? Let's see if we can make it better, shall we?"

He and Bob Parker went into a treatment room to examine the cairn. The rest of them stayed behind and petted Denny.

"When I saw him lying on the road, so still, I was so sure he was going to die," Gina said. "Doesn't he look brilliant now?"

"Fantastic!" agreed Neil. "You're going to be better in no time, aren't you, Denny?"

Denny barked his agreement and gave everyone a good lick.

Soon Mike Turner and Bob Parker returned.

"How's the cairn?" asked Neil.

"Just a cut," said the vet. "It was quite deep, but fortunately it wasn't infected. I've put a stitch in it and you can take him home again. He'll be fine."

"Thank you for all you've done for Denny," said Gina. "Can I take him home now?"

"I'm afraid not," Mike Turner told her. "I want to keep him in tonight, just for observation."

"Oh." Gina's face fell. "Why?"

"He's had a nasty bang," said Mike Turner. "I want to be quite sure he's fit before you take him."

Gina pulled a disappointed face but she knew it was for the best.

"Your dad's told me about Sugar and Spice," Mike Turner said to Neil. "Don't worry, if anyone comes in with two new Westies, I'll be on to them straight away. And I'll ask all my clients if they've seen them, too."

"And don't forget to ask everyone you meet if they can give a home to Billy," Neil reminded him.

*

Neil and Emily couldn't eat much dinner that night. They were both feeling too sad about Billy and too worried about Sugar and Spice. Not one single person had rung about Billy, and the police hadn't phoned to say they'd found the Westies.

As they sat around the kitchen table, and with Sam snoozing in his basket, Neil and Emily went down their list of people who they thought could have stolen the Westies.

"We thought Mike Turner might know someone whose Westie has died," said Emily.

"Oh yes, and then what would you do?" asked Carole Parker.

"We could ring them up . . ." began Emily.

"And ask them if they've stolen Sugar and Spice?" she asked. "They'll love you for that!"

"No," said Neil. He'd been giving it some real thought. "We could pretend we're ringing to see if they could give a home to Billy, but while we're talking to them, we could listen to see if we hear any dogs in the background."

"But even if you do, they might not be Sugar and Spice," said Carole. "They might have bought a new dog, or they could be looking after one for a neighbour. They could have visitors, it could even be a dog on the television."

"It's a good idea, Neil," said his dad. "But we can't really use information from the vet in that way. If any of his clients have got new Westies, he'll see them soon enough."

Neil frowned. He didn't even cheer up when someone rang the doorbell. He wasn't going to get his hopes raised for nothing again.

It was Dave.

"I just called to ask how Denny was," he said.

"He's doing fine. It's nice of you to enquire," said Carole. "Emily, would you like to make Mr Thomas a cup of coffee?"

"That would be very nice. Thanks a lot!" Dave accepted cheerfully. "It was good to have an excuse to come round here, actually. I love dogs."

"You're welcome to look round the

kennels any time," said Mr Parker.

Sam got up and padded over to Dave, sniffing at his shoes and trousers.

Dave patted the Border collie's head. "He's a lovely dog," he said. "You know, I used to have a dog. When I was a kid I had a black one with a white patch over one eye. Buster, his name was. Oh, he was smashing. Such a good friend to me. We used to go everywhere together."

"What happened to him?" asked Sarah.

Dave pulled a sad face. "Oh, he grew old and died." He shook his head. "I was pretty upset at the time. I did think about getting another for a while."

"When one dog dies, you have to get another," said Neil passionately. "And we've got just the dog for you here. He's called Billy . . ."

Dave stood up, shaking his head. "Oh no," he said. "I can't have another dog. Not now. I'm out all day."

"You could!" said Neil. "He'd go everywhere with you, just like Buster did. You can't beat a dog as a companion. Always waiting for you, giving you so much love . . ."

Dave shook his head again. "Thanks, anyway. I'd like to see the dogs, though."

Hope flared in Neil as he led Dave out to the rescue centre. Billy stood up and panted excitedly, his head in its normal tilted position as he made his one eye do the work of two. Neil saw how Dave grinned at him.

"You're a lovely boy, aren't you?" Dave said to Billy.

Neil opened the pen so that Dave could stroke Billy's shiny black head and scratch behind his ears. He was rewarded with a loving lick on the wrist.

"Well, what do you think?" Neil asked, then held his breath, waiting for Dave's

answer. He and Billy obviously liked each other.

"Sorry," said Dave. "He's a smashing dog but I'm sure someone else more suitable will want to give him a home."

Neil couldn't hide his disappointment.

That night, Neil lay in bed feeling angry with the whole world: with the thieves who'd stolen Sugar and Spice; with the monster who had ill-treated Billy; and with every one of the millions of people out there who didn't want to adopt Billy. What was wrong with them all?

One thing Neil hated was having a mystery he couldn't solve. Over and over again, he tried to imagine who could possibly have crept in and snatched the Westies from under their noses. How was it they hadn't barked as they were being taken away?

The thieves certainly hadn't come the front way and carried Sugar and Spice past the house, or Sam would have barked, even if the Parkers themselves hadn't heard the Westies. That meant they must have come through the front gate and gone out across the exercise field and the woods. It had to be someone who knew the area well. Someone from around Compton. Maybe someone they knew.

And Neil had to find out – fast.

Chapter Eight

Neil's brilliant idea hit him in the early hours of the morning. He sat up suddenly and immediately glanced at his bedside alarm clock. It was half past five and he was going to need help.

He dressed quickly and padded into Emily's bedroom.

He shook his sister awake and explained the plan.

"What can you hear outside, Em?" Neil was obviously excited.

"Nothing. A few birds, perhaps," she replied sleepily.

"Exactly! Nothing! Sugar and Spice were

the noisiest dogs we've ever had! They're bound to be equally noisy wherever they are! So what better time to go out looking for them than at the crack of dawn on a Sunday morning!"

"Brilliant idea!" she cried, suddenly waking up.

"Right, then. Get your coat and we're outta here!"

Neil and Emily set off, full of hope. They cycled along the deserted roads, looking and listening. It was amazing just how many sounds there were. Birds sang from the treetops and the leaves rustled in the wind.

They covered some old ground again, places where they had already looked unsuccessfully.

After half an hour the countryside was beginning to get noisier. It was becoming more difficult for them to hear other sounds beyond the drone of cars and bleating sheep. Neil sighed and looked at his watch. In twelve hours' time, Mr and Mrs Jepson would be coming to collect two little dogs who weren't there . . .

Neil dismounted from his bike and propped it up against a drystone wall. He flopped down into the green grass underneath and leaned back.

"Let's think really hard about this," said Neil.

Emily sat on the wall and dangled her feet.

"We've looked everywhere, Neil."

"Where could someone put two noisy dogs and not hear them barking?"

"It would have to be somewhere fairly soundproof, or away from roads and houses," said Emily. "Like a farm building in the middle of nowhere, or even a shed at the bottom of a long garden."

"Or a garage."

"I think we should go further into town and look for places like that."

"Yes," said Neil. "And we need to be more daring. We need to look over a few fences and sneak into some gardens!"

"Now you're talking!"

At first, excitement kept them going. Neil and Emily cycled down little lanes they never knew existed, calling out the names of the two missing dogs and hoping for a high-pitched response.

Their spirits were lifted when they found an old disused Victorian water tower and heard some yapping. Then they saw a woman come down the lane from behind it with two spaniel pups on leads, and they were bitterly disappointed.

"We've got to keep looking," urged Neil. He could sense Emily was beginning to get downhearted. "Let's try just a few more places, OK?"

"OK, Neil. Just a few more."

Woodland Way was the highest street in Compton. The long gardens of the houses backed on to the hillside and were very steep. Most people had carved them into terraces and planted borders of flowers and shrubs, but one, at the furthest end, still had a wild, overgrown garden, so that it looked like a piece of the woodland beyond.

Slowly, Emily and Neil wheeled their bikes along the quiet road. Somewhere in the far distance they could hear barking.

"Do you hear that, Neil?" Emily asked her brother.

He stopped in his tracks. "Hear what?"

"It's a long way away. Maybe I didn't hear anything . . ."

"Hey, wait a minute!" Neil put his finger to his lips. "I heard it then. If it's coming from the top of the hill, we'll never get up there before whoever is there has gone!"

"We could take a short cut, through the woods . . ." Emily suggested.

"What would we do with our bikes?"

"Why don't we leave them right up by the far wall of that end garden? I'm sure they'd be OK for a while. There's nobody around," said Emily.

With difficulty, they pushed the bikes up the steep, rocky ground that rose from the end of the street. As they followed the high garden wall, which was old and quite crumbly in places and overhung with trees, they heard the barking again. Only louder!

"Neil!" Emily whispered. "I think it's coming from in there!"

She pointed to the garden.

"Right. I'm climbing up to take a look!"

Neil propped his bike against the wall and searched for a foothold on the mossy stones. With difficulty, he levered himself up – and found himself gazing at a large stone outbuilding. It had a door and a window and was built as solidly as any house.

"Emily, I'm going over," he said and silently slipped down into the wild garden.

There was a narrow set of stone steps winding down from the outbuilding, but there were so many bushes and tall trees in the way that you couldn't see much of the house it led to. Knowing that he couldn't be seen made Neil feel less scared as he pushed his way through the thistles and nettles towards the building.

The yapping started again. It was quite frenzied. He was dying to call the dogs' names, but didn't want to risk being heard by the occupants of the house.

The window was very dirty. He spat on it and rubbed it with his sleeve. It was dark inside but he could just make out two small white shapes jumping up and down like jack-in-the-boxes as they barked their heads off.

Neil clambered back up the wall, leaned over the top and told Emily the good news. "They're here! We've found them!"

"Let me come over, too," she said.

She scrambled up and dropped over the wall amongst the dock leaves and tall grass on the other side.

"Ugh, nettles!" she shuddered.

Neil picked up a long twig and pushed the waist-high nettles aside so that his sister could get through.

"They're in here," said Neil.

Emily wasn't as cautious as Neil had been. She banged on the window calling "Sugar! Spice!", ignoring her brother's pleas to keep her voice down.

A shower of familiar barking told them that they really had found Sugar and Spice. All they had to do now was liberate them.

"We've got to get them out, and we've got to do it now." Neil's voice was very determined.

The stout wooden door was firmly locked and the window obviously hadn't been opened for years. It was sealed shut with layers of ancient paint. The Westies were trying vainly to push their little button noses under the door.

Neil stepped back and scratched his head. "Emily, I wonder if you can get round the back of this thing?"

The building backed up against the garden wall and was almost part of it. By climbing up the sloping earth at the side, he could get on to the roof, which was covered with old, mossy slates.

"Careful, Neil!"

"I'm OK. I've made it up." Neil bent back

one of the rusty pins holding a slate in place. It was easily removed and he flung it silently into the long grass below. Then he removed a second, and a third. Below, he found a sheet of something tarry and nasty – waterproofing to stop the rain getting in if the tiles leaked. He needed a knife to break through.

Neil thought of his bike saddlebag. He carried some cycle tools and he knew he had a screwdriver. Maybe he would be able to pierce the roof lining with that.

He asked Emily to find it. She threw it up to him and he managed to remove four more slates from the back of the roof and jab holes in the stiff material beneath them. It left a jagged tear just big enough for him to drop through.

Neil was in luck. He landed on some sacking and it only took him a few moments to get his breath back. The two Westies were all over him, scrabbling at his legs, licking his ankles. He gave them a swift pat, then went over to the door. It had been padlocked on the outside so there was no way of opening it. Apart from some saucers of food and water for the dogs, there was nothing much else. A few old garden tools lay propped up against the back wall in the shadows, but there was nothing to stand on that would be high enough for him to get out the way he had come. He was trapped.

Then he heard Emily's voice, calling urgently through the hole in the roof. "Neil, Neil, get out quick! Someone's coming!"

Chapter Nine

Emily must have managed to hide in time because Neil didn't hear any further shouts or conversation. Footsteps were heading purposefully up the steps towards the door. Inside the shed, panic surged in his throat and he flattened himself against the wall on the side where the door would be opened.

"Well here you are, then," said a grumpy female voice as the door was unlocked and pushed open just a crack. "I don't see why I've got to feed you two noisy horrors. Still, it's only until tomorrow, then good riddance!"

The saucers, piled high with dog food, were almost hurled in, and the door slammed shut again. Maybe the woman had been scared the dogs might run off if she opened the door too wide. Neil had never been so relieved in his life. But what had she meant by "It's only until tomorrow, then good riddance"? What were they planning to do with Sugar and Spice then? Whatever it was, it didn't sound good and it was even more vital that he and Emily found a way of getting the Westies back home immediately! But how?

It was Emily who came up with the brilliant idea. She scrambled up the back wall and spoke to Neil through the hole in the roof.

"You know my bike panniers? If I lowered them through this hole using the straps, you could put Sugar and Spice in and I could pull them out!"

Neil whistled in admiration. "Good thinking, Em."

A few minutes later the panniers came dangling down through the hole.

"I can't reach!" Neil called to his sister.

"I'll lie down then and stretch my arms through," whispered Emily. She was trying to keep her voice down, knowing that there was definitely somebody in the house.

Neil had to jump a bit, but he managed to put Spice, and then Sugar, into a pannier each. He couldn't do up the strap to fasten them in – he just had to hope that they wouldn't fall out.

But Emily got them safely up. He could hear her scrabbling and panting as she scrambled back off the roof and over the back wall. He heard her saying calming words to the two dogs as she fixed the panniers back on to her bike.

That left just him, alone in the shed, and he had to find a way out somehow. There was no way that Emily could haul him out, too!

He used the screwdriver to scrape around one of the windows. Even when he'd chipped out a considerable amount of paint, dirt and old spider webs, it still wouldn't budge. He started chiselling at the putty which was holding the pane of glass in the frame. To his surprise it came away easily as it was very crumbly. He loosened all the way round – then suddenly, to his horror, the glass fell outwards and landed on the stone paving slabs at the top of the steps with a loud splintering crash.

From the other end of the hilly garden, he heard a door grate open and a woman shout, "Who's there?"

The window was a tight squeeze. He came out head first, managing to avoid the broken glass. Leaping to his feet, he saw the woman coming slowly up the steps towards him.

He hurled himself at the wall and was up and over before she'd finished shouting, "Hey, you! Stop!"

"Quick, Em!" he shouted. "Are the dogs secure?"

"Yes!" she yelled.

They pushed off, their bikes bouncing over rocks and stones.

As they sped down Woodland Way, they could hear the woman shouting after them, but they didn't pause for breath until they got onto the Compton Road. They stopped to check that Sugar and Spice were all right after such a bumpy ride. Then, at a slower pace, they set off up the hill towards home.

"That was close!" said Emily.

"Wasn't it just!"

"Do you think we ought to go to the police first?" Emily asked Neil.

"No," said Neil. He sounded very confident. "I think we should get them home, have them checked over by the vet, and then get them washed and brushed and looking good for the Jepsons."

Neil and Emily had never felt more relieved in their lives when they opened the gate to King Street Kennels and rode up the drive towards their house. Before they'd even dismounted, with Sugar and Spice still nestling in the panniers, Carole Parker came rushing out of the house towards them, waving a piece of paper.

"Look what I've found! It was under the mat. Goodness knows how long it's been there. I found it when I was cleaning the hall. I picked the mat up to shake it and there it was," she said breathlessly.

Neil and Emily looked at the piece of

paper. It was only a short message, very
badly spelt.

Dont wory about the dogs.
There OK.
We've only borowed them.
We'll bring them bak.

"As soon as your father comes in, I'm
going to ask him if we should give this to
the police," said Mrs Parker. "It's vital
evidence."

"Yes, it is," replied Neil, turning the
paper over. There was nothing on the other
side. It was just a jagged scrap, torn along
one edge.

"But there's no need. Look!" said Neil.

Emily unfastened a strap, delved into
one of her panniers and brought out a very
confused-looking Spice. Out of the other,
she produced Sugar.

They had never seen their mother look
so amazed. "Where did you find them?"
she asked.

"In Woodland Way, at the very last
house. They were shut in a big shed. I had
to break in to get them," Neil confessed.

"You can tell me all about it after we've taken this pair round to the kennels and got them safely shut in. We've got a couple of hours before the Jepsons are due. Neil, will you ring Mike Turner and see if he's free to check them over? We can't give them back to Mr and Mrs Jepson without knowing if they're OK. Emily, we'll go and find Kate. See you in a moment, Neil."

Neil rang the vet, who said he'd be there in half an hour.

Neil sat down to study the piece of paper. It wasn't necessary now as a clue – they knew where the dogs had been kept – but there was something about it that was bothering him.

The ink was a funny colour, a sort of purple-blue. He'd seen that colour before somewhere . . .

Just then, his father drew up in the Range Rover. Instead of rushing out to meet him and tell him the news, Neil ran up the stairs to his bedroom. There, in the rucksack he used for school, was the exercise book containing Lucy's history notes which, in all the excitement of Friday's radio programme, he had forgotten to give back.

The ink was the identical colour! The writing looked different, but it was probably disguised. The loop on the "g" of "dogs" was exactly the same, and so was the way the "t"s were crossed.

But that spelling . . . Lucy was consistently top in spelling tests. Maybe she'd done it to try and disguise the fact that the note was written by her. He couldn't be absolutely certain, but, despite the spelling, he was at least ninety per cent sure that it was Lucy who had written that note. He didn't know where their new house was. Jack had mentioned something about "up near the woods", but Neil couldn't remember hearing the name of the road.

He ran downstairs with the exercise book and heard a clamour outside as his father and Sarah were brought up to date with the happy news.

He heard the word "police" mentioned several times. Then his father came striding through the door.

"No, Dad!" he ordered, blocking his father's route to the telephone.

"What do you mean, 'no'? Of course the police have to be informed. These dog thieves have to be arrested!" Bob Parker protested.

"There's no need. I'm pretty sure I know who took them. It was Lucy and Jack Vaughan from my school!"

Bob Parker stared at Neil in astonishment.

"But they're your friends!" he said. "How could friends of yours do a thing like that?"

Neil shook his head, then showed his father the note.

"I believe they only borrowed them and didn't intend to keep them," he assured his dad. "I bet they're thinking someone has stolen Sugar and Spice from them! We'd better go round and see them, before *they* go to the police and report the Westies stolen!"

Chapter Ten

Neil's father introduced himself to the woman who opened the door. "I'm Bob Parker, from King Street Kennels. Are you Mrs Vaughan?"

"Yes. If you've come for Sugar and Spice, I've . . . I've got some bad news," she said hesitantly. "Someone's stolen them. They got through our shed roof."

"I know," Neil announced, coming forward. "It was me. I took them!"

Mrs Vaughan's jaw dropped open. She went white.

"I'm sorry, I don't understand. Why didn't you just come round to the front door and ask for them?"

"We didn't know that this was your new house," said Emily. There was another glimmer of recognition as Mrs Vaughan recognized the other dog-napper.

Bob Parker was trying to work out why Mrs Vaughan assumed they knew the dogs were with her.

"Sugar and Spice were missing, Mrs Vaughan," said Neil. "We heard them bark, and we had to break into the shed and get them back!"

"What do you mean, missing?" Mrs Vaughan frowned. "You knew all along they were here! You asked my children to look after them!"

"Excuse me?" Bob Parker couldn't believe his ears.

"And what little terrors they were! Awful dogs. Absolutely awful. They chewed our new sofa, made a mess on the carpet and, worst of all, they've got fleas! I couldn't believe it! That's why I had to shut them in the shed. Not to mention the neighbours complaining about their dreadful barking . . ."

"Er, Mum . . ." Lucy Vaughan had crept timidly up behind her mother, her face red and tear-stained.

"Let me explain, Lucy," insisted Jack, pushing her aside and facing the Parkers. "We lied to Mum. We told her your kennels were over-booked and that you'd asked us to look after Sugar and Spice over the weekend."

"What on earth possessed you to do that?" his mother exploded.

"You know how much we wanted a dog? And how you said Billy would be too big? You only liked little dogs, you said. Well, we thought that if we borrowed Sugar and Spice and took them home, you'd think they were really OK after all. We thought you might let us have a small dog," Jack confessed.

"But it didn't work because they were such trouble," Lucy chimed in, looking at Neil and Emily. "We left you the note so that you wouldn't be worried, but you wouldn't know it was us."

"We didn't find it till today. I think Sam must have pushed it under the mat," Neil said.

Bob Parker was lost for words. "You two have caused so much trouble," he told Lucy and Jack. "Do you realize what this might have meant for the kennels? The owner of Sugar and Spice is on Compton Council and he's due to collect the dogs tonight. Imagine how he'd have reacted if they weren't there!"

Lucy and Jack both looked guilty.

"We didn't think . . ." Jack began, meeting Neil's eyes guiltily.

"*Mrs* Jepson would have been even worse," said Neil.

"Look what you put the Parker family through! I hope you're going to say you're sorry!" snapped their mother.

"Sorry," they both whispered.

"We'll never do anything like this again," Jack promised Neil's dad, his face glum. "There's no point. There's no chance of Mum ever letting us have a dog now!"

"I feel sorry for Jack and Lucy," Mr Parker said as he drove Neil and Emily home. "It's obvious that they love dogs and would care for one very well – if only their mother would give in. Look, Neil, why don't you invite them round soon? If their mother drove them over here, I could invite her to have a look round the kennels. You never know, maybe it would change her mind – make her see that not all dogs are as destructive and badly behaved as Sugar and Spice."

"Does this mean you've forgiven them, Dad?" Neil asked.

"Of course I have. It was a kind of cry for help from two dog-loving young people. Even if it was a rather misguided one," replied his dad.

"Why don't I invite them round after school tomorrow, to help me exercise Sam?" suggested Neil.

His father thought it was a great idea. "Right, you two," he said as they got out of the car. "I can see Mike Turner has arrived. He's probably given Sugar and Spice the once-over by now. I'll just go and talk to him about them."

Neil and Emily went out to the kennels and found their mother holding Spice while Kate brushed him. Sarah was clutching the bows which Sugar and Spice had been wearing when the Jepsons had brought them to the kennels.

"I'm going to tie their bows on and make them look pretty," she announced proudly.

Neil and Emily looked at each other and winced at the thought, remembering how they'd rushed to take the ghastly bows off as soon as the Jepsons had left!

Neil left them there and went back to the house. He wanted to walk Sam and have an excuse for not being around when the Jepsons arrived. He could hear his father still talking to Mike Turner in the lounge, and popped his head round the door.

His dad greeted him with a broad smile. "About Billy . . . Mike and I may have come up with an idea."

"You mean you're going to have him, Mike? That would be fantastic!" Neil said enthusiastically.

"No, not me, I'm afraid. But I think we've found a way of postponing what's due to happen tomorrow, to give him more of a chance."

Mike was clutching some booklets and Bob Parker had a triumphant grin on his face.

"When I checked the Westies over I found that they were very obese. They also had bad infestations of fleas and mites. It was obvious that their owners had never thought of de-fleaing them. Heaven knows what their house must be like. You see, dog and cat fleas often drop off the animal and make nests in the carpet or in soft furnishings like chairs and sofas. They hop back on to the host animal for a meal, then hop back to their nests again."

"But if the animal is away for some time, the fleas get very hungry, and that's when they hop on humans and get a meal from us instead!" said Bob.

"So the Jepsons are likely to get savaged by a horde of fleas the moment they walk through their door?" asked Neil, his lips twitching in amusement at the thought.

"Probably!" chuckled Mike. "I'm going to recommend that they stay here for a week, while we get their diet and their skin problems under control and start obedience training."

Oh, no! thought Neil.

"Here's the rest of the plan," said Bob Parker. "Once Mike has got Mr Jepson suitably embarrassed about the state of his own dogs, I'm going to tell him about your radio broadcast, and point out how the voters would react if they came flocking to offer Billy a home, only to find that I'd put him down because I had to stick too closely to his strict Council rules."

"I can't wait to see their faces! I'm going to stick around and watch!" said Neil.

"I hardly think they'd elect Jepson again next time round, would they?"

At five past six, the Jepsons' car arrived. Mrs Jepson climbed out. She was wearing a tight suit in the brightest shade of pink Neil had ever seen.

"Where are my little poochy-poos?" she said, looking disappointed that her dogs weren't already straining on the leads to greet her.

"They're in their pen," said Carole Parker briskly. "You can come and see them."

"What do you mean, 'see them'? Aren't they ready to be brought home?" said Mr Jepson.

Neil and Emily exchanged glances. How were their parents going to handle this?

"I think Mike Turner, the vet, would like a word with you," said Bob Parker.

"My babies!" she gasped. "Has something happened to them? Oh, my poor babies!"

"They're quite all right. It's just that the vet came on a routine kennel inspection and noticed one or two things about your dogs," Carole explained.

"What do you mean?" snapped Mr Jepson. "We look after our dogs perfectly well – there's nothing wrong with them. Look here, if you think that—"

He didn't get a chance to finish because at that moment Mike Turner came out of the house.

"Ah, hello. Just the people I wanted to see. I'd like you to take a look at this booklet. It's all about the risk to a dog's health of giving them the wrong diet. Now, I've had a look at Sugar and Spice's teeth. It seems they've been given rather a lot of sweets recently . . ."

Mrs Jepson blushed. "They do love their sweeties," she admitted.

"I'm sure they do, but they're very bad for them. You love your dogs, don't you?"

"Oh yes. More than anything!" Mrs Jepson said breathlessly.

"And you do want them to live to a ripe old age?" the vet continued.

"Of course!" Mrs Jepson was hanging on to his every word. "If anything happened to my two babies . . ." She left the sentence unfinished as she dabbed her eyes with her handkerchief.

Now Mike fixed his eyes on Mr Jepson. "I'll be frank with you," he said. "If Sugar and Spice don't stick to the diet they've been on since they came to King Street Kennels, and get more exercise, I wouldn't give them much more than two more years. Their obesity is a strain on their hearts and it will kill them."

Mrs Jepson gasped and clutched her husband's arm. Neil knew Mike was getting through to them.

"And, whereas most dogs get the odd flea from time to time, these two were badly infested," the vet continued. "They need regular de-fleaing. All dogs and cats do. I've got another leaflet for you to read on that. Now, I've already started them on the necessary vitamin tablets. It will improve their skin condition."

"What skin condition?" asked Mr

Jepson. His stern expression had given way to sheepishness.

"The one caused by their flea infestation and their dietary deficiencies. Don't worry, though . . ." Mike Turner's voice softened when he saw how upset Mrs Jepson was looking, "they'll be all right. But I've recommended that they stay here for another few days, until their diet and treatment begin to work."

Mrs Jepson looked as if she was about to cry. "But I do so want to take them home with me," she said, her voice a bit wobbly.

"I think we should do what the vet says, dear," said her husband, putting an arm round his wife.

"Can I see them now, please?" Mrs Jepson asked faintly. Neil felt rather sorry for her. He could tell that the Westies really were her whole life.

They all went round to the kennels. Kate had Sugar and Spice out of the pen on their leads. The two dogs jumped up at Mrs Jepson and scraped their dirty paws all over the hem of her skirt.

"Naughty babies!" exclaimed Mrs Jepson.

"Ah! That's another thing I wanted to talk to you about," said Mike Turner. "Obedience training. How would you like it if they started doing what you told them? The Parkers run classes every Wednesday and Sunday."

While Mike was explaining dog training to Mrs Jepson, Mr Parker had drawn Mr Jepson aside. Then they started walking off in the direction of the rescue centre. When Neil finally managed to catch up with them, he found them with Billy. Mr Jepson was actually stroking him.

"Yes, yes, he's a fine dog. I do agree with you that he deserves a good home. I'll talk to my colleagues in the morning. I feel sure they can bend the rules, especially with the radio programme going out tomorrow. It wouldn't make Compton Council look good in the eyes of the town if we had the poor thing put down, would it?"

Neil smiled at last. Billy had a chance. One last chance.

The following day after school Mrs Vaughan arrived at King Street Kennels with Lucy and Jack.

"It's the dogs' feeding time," Neil pointed out, as he welcomed them all and tried to explain why there was so much noise. "It's deafening, isn't it?"

"You lot go on. I'll stay here," said Mrs Vaughan.

Lucy looked disappointed. "Oh, please come too, Mum!" she begged and looked delighted when her mother said, "Oh, all right then."

They found Sarah with Kate.

"Who wants to measure out Sugar and Spice's diet?" asked Kate.

Lucy volunteered. Sarah thought their little meals were very funny. "They're not getting much more than I give Fudge!" she giggled.

"That hamster of yours needs putting on a diet, too!" Kate warned her. "He's so fat, he'll get stuck in his exercise wheel one of these days!"

"That one's very quiet!" exclaimed Jack. It was the little cairn terrier, waiting patiently for his dinner. Unlike the other dogs, he didn't bark. Instead, he waited politely with his tongue hanging out and his stubby tail wagging.

"He's so sweet! What's his name?" asked Lucy.

"He hasn't got one. He's a stray. We're waiting to see if his owner turns up. If he or she doesn't, then we'll try and find him a new home."

"Why has he got that bandage round his paw?" asked Mrs Vaughan.

"He'd hurt his leg. The lady at Badger's Farm found him," Emily explained.

Kate opened the cage door and put down the dish. "Sit," she ordered. The cairn sat and made no attempt to touch his dinner, although his mouth was drooling.

"Right, go!" said Kate. The dog began to lap up the food in his bowl.

"I don't think we'll have much trouble finding a home for this one," Kate said. "He's a perfect house dog."

Lucy and Jack looked at their mother. Mrs Vaughan consulted her watch and said, "Come on, we'd better be going."

Neil was disappointed for them. But then, just before they drove off, Neil was sure he heard Mrs Vaughan say, "Just give me a couple of days to think about it, will you?"

He suddenly had a funny feeling that Lucy and Jack might not be without a dog for much longer.

That evening, the Parkers glued themselves to the radio to hear *Tell Tony*.

"Gosh, you were good!" Emily said admiringly.

"Yes, Neil, you were terrific," agreed his mother.

"I didn't even think about what I was saying. It just came out," Neil told them.

"Straight from the heart," said his dad.

Neil wasn't the blushing type, but he did feel a faint heat sweeping over his face and swiftly took Sam out for his evening walk. He hated people making a fuss, especially when the object of their attention was him!

The day after the radio programme was broadcast, the kennels received several long-awaited enquiries about Billy. Kate took their details and sifted through the most promising. She made a string of appointments for the following day with the people who seemed in the best position to offer him a good home.

In the evening, the Parkers were just finishing their dinner when the calm was suddenly broken by the sound of a van on the gravel drive.

"It's Dave! I wonder what he wants?" cried Neil, rushing to open the door as a hot, dishevelled-looking Dave climbed down from the driver's seat.

"Am I too late?" he asked. "Only I had to pick up some tyres from York today. It's taken me hours to get back."

"Too late for what?" asked Emily.

"For Billy! Has anyone else been to get him? Don't tell me he's gone already?"

"No!" said Neil. "He's still here – just! Why? Don't tell me you want him after all?" He was beginning to smile.

"Too right I do," said Dave. "Ever since I saw him, I've been going over and over what you said about a dog being the best kind of companion. I knew you were right. And when I heard you on the radio . . . well, that made my mind up for me good and proper. I had no idea he was about to be destroyed. All day, while I've been driving around, I've been tortured by thoughts of Billy being put to sleep, and I knew I couldn't let it happen. Can I have him?"

"I can't think of anyone better to have Billy," said Carole Parker. "Can anyone else?"

"No!" said everyone.

Dave's face lit up. "You'll have to remind me of everything I'll need for him. It's been a long time," he said as they all went off to the rescue centre.

It was as though Billy knew that Dave had come for him. As soon as Neil opened the kennel door, Billy ignored him and Emily and bounded straight over to Dave, jumping up at him, barking excitedly.

Dave didn't say a word. He just stroked the big black dog, fondling him behind his ears, patting him on the back and stroking his head.

Dave looked up, grinning. "He's wonderful. Aren't you, Billy?"

Billy barked loudly.

"I'm really glad you came back for him," said Neil.

They all stood in the driveway, ready to wave Billy and Dave off. As Dave climbed into his van, Billy sat proudly in the passenger seat, gazing out of the window, as though he'd always sat there.

"I'll bring him back to see you," called Dave, as he drove off.

"You'd better!" cried Neil.

Sarah wiped her eyes.

"Don't cry, darling," said her dad.

"Billy's gone to a good home – there's no reason to be sad."

"I'm not sad," sniffed Sarah.

Emily and Neil smiled. They felt just the same.

PUPPY PATROL titles available from
Macmillan Children's Books

The prices shown below are correct at the time of going to press.
However, Macmillan Publishers reserve the right to show new retail
prices on covers which may differ from those previously advertised.

JENNY DALE

1. Teacher's Pet	0 330 34905 8	£2.99
2. Big Ben	0 330 34906 6	£2.99
3. Abandoned!	0 330 34907 4	£2.99
4. Double Trouble	0 330 34908 2	£2.99
5. Star Paws	0 330 34909 0	£2.99
6. Tug of Love	0 330 34910 4	£2.99
7. Saving Skye	0 330 35492 2	£2.99
8. Tuff's Luck	0 330 35493 0	£2.99
9. Red Alert	0 330 36937 7	£2.99
10. The Great Escape	0 330 36938 5	£2.99
11. Perfect Puppy	0 330 36939 3	£2.99
12. Sam and Delilah	0 330 36940 7	£2.99
13. The Sea Dog	0 330 37039 1	£2.99
14. Puppy School	0 330 37040 5	£2.99
15. A Winter's Tale	0 330 37041 3	£2.99
16. Puppy Love	0 330 37042 1	£2.99
17. Best of Friends	0 330 37043 X	£2.99
18. King of the Castle	0 330 37392 7	£2.99
19. Posh Pup	0 330 37393 5	£2.99
20. Charlie's Choice	0 330 37394 3	£2.99

All Macmillan titles can be ordered at your local bookshop
or are available by post from:

Book Service by Post
PO Box 29, Douglas, Isle of Man IM99 1BQ

Credit cards accepted. For details:
Telephone: 01624 675137
Fax: 01624 670923
E-mail: bookshop@enterprise.net

Free postage and packing in the UK.
Overseas customers: add £1 per book (paperback)
and £3 per book (hardback).